For Alys and her mum . . . always —M. S.

For George and Charlie —A. B.

First published in Great Britain in January 2017 by Bloomsbury Publishing Plc
Published in the United States of America in January 2017
by Bloomsbury Children's Books
www.bloomsbury.com

For information about permission to reproduce selections from this book, write to
Permissions, Bloomsbury Children's Books, 1385 Broadway, New York, New York 10018
Bloomsbury books may be purchased for business or promotional use. For information on bulk purchases please contact
Macmillan Corporate and Premium Sales Department at specialmarkets@macmillan.com

Library of Congress Cataloging-in-Publication Data
available upon request
ISBN 978-1-68119-345-8 (hardcover) • ISBN 978-1-68119-346-5 (e-book) • ISBN 978-1-68119-347-2 (e-PDF)

Art created with acrylic paint and colored pencil
Typeset in Garden Pro
Book design by Kristina Coates
Printed in China by Leo Paper Products, Heshan, Guangdong
2 4 6 8 10 9 7 5 3 1

All papers used by Bloomsbury Publishing, Inc., are natural, recyclable products made from wood grown in well-managed forests. The manufacturing processes conform to the environmental regulations of the country of origin.

I'll Love You Always

Mark Sperring

illustrated by Alison Brown

BLOOMSBURY

NEW YORK LONDON OXFORD NEW DELHI SYDNEY

How long will I love you?
A second is too short.
A second is no time
for a love of this sort.

A minute is no better, for minutes fly by!

They're gone in a moment like a sweet butterfly.

An hour's still nothing—
it whirls by so fast.

I'll love you much longer than hours can last.

A morning is so brief,
an afternoon, too.

From sunrise to sunset,
I'll keep loving you.

Will I love you when night falls?

Of course, and beyond . . .

Will I love you tomorrow?
Oh yes, on and on . . .

I'll love you for whole days
stretched out in a line.

I'll love you for weeks
and a much longer time!

I'll love you for months
heaped up to the sky.

I'll love you through seasons
as they bluster by.

I'll love you for whole years
and though things might change . . .
as you grow bigger
my love stays the same.

How long will I love you?
If you need to know,
I'll tuck you in tightly,
then whisper it low . . .

I'll love you for years and for
months, weeks, and days.
I'll love you for hours
and minutes . . .

. . . always.

I'll love you forever, not one second less.
For that is what mommies and daddies do best.

I'll love you forever, not one second less.
For that is what mommies and daddies do best.